Lara was tucked up in her cosy bed. It was time
to close her eyes and sink into sweet dreams.

But Lara couldn't sleep. She lay awake missing her Nana
and thinking sad thoughts that had no name or shape.

She thought of all the Sundays spent at the
beach with Nana, how they always held hands,
and the way she smelled like strawberries.

The thoughts swirled around and around inside
her and spilled out into tears that were
heavy with blue.

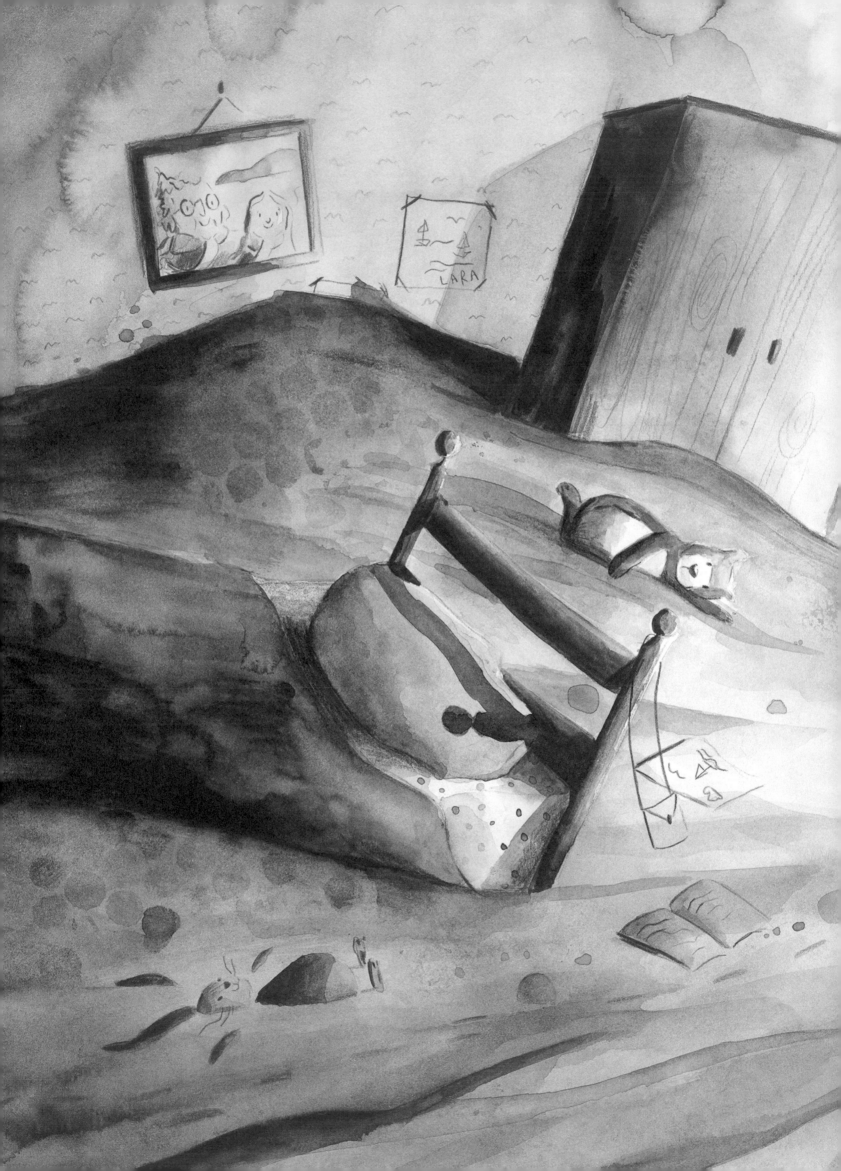

Drop by drop they filled up the
room until there was no space
left to hold them.

Out of her house, past the park and down
the street her tears carried her, leaving behind
all that Lara knew and loved.

Until she floated far, far away…

...out to sea.

Lara drifted alone through the night and
into days and weeks. And she soon forgot
everything that made her feel
happy or safe.

She could no longer remember the smell of
strawberries or the touch of Nana's warm hand.

There was nothing but the cold swirling sea.

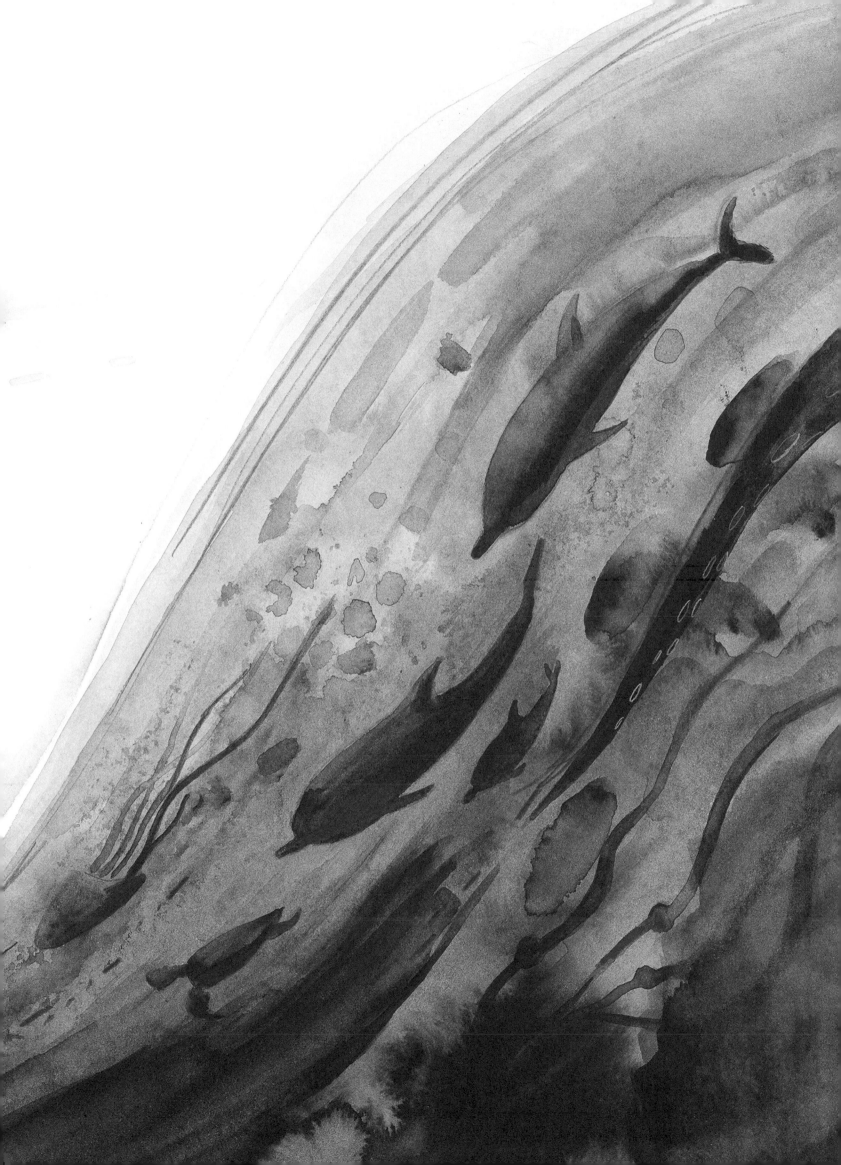

But then, deep in the dark belly of the ocean,
Lara saw something softly shimmer.

A glowing pearl, waiting just for her.

She clasped it in her fingers, pressed it close to her heart,
and realised that not all things had been washed away.

It was then, when
Lara looked up, that
she could see she
was not alone.

Lara remembered the things in her life that still glowed
with light and love. She pictured her Nana and smiled.

With her pearl safely tucked in her pocket,
Lara picked up her oars and set off towards home.

This would not be Lara's last time out to sea.
There would be other sleepless nights
and sad goodbyes.

But Lara knew she was not alone and would
always find her way back home.

For those who always join me out at sea:
Wesley, Zara, Mum & Dad.

First published in the United Kingdom in 2021 by Thames & Hudson Ltd,
181A High Holborn, London WC1V 7QX
This paperback edition 2022

Out to Sea © 2021 Thames & Hudson Ltd, London
Text and Illustrations © 2021 Helen Kellock

Copyedited by Sarah Stewart

British Library Cataloguing-in-Publication Data
A catalogue record for this book is available from the British Library

ISBN 978-0-500-66014-0

Printed and bound in Belgium by Graphius

Be the first to know about our new releases,
exclusive content and author events by visiting
thamesandhudson.com
thamesandhudsonusa.com
thamesandhudson.com.au